The Tender Art of Holding On

Hatty Jones

Published by Hatty Jones, 2024.

THE TENDER ART OF HOLDING ON

First edition. October 21, 2024.

Copyright © 2024 Hatty Jones.

ISBN: 979-8227751416

Written by Hatty Jones.

The Tender Art of Holding On

The Tender Art of Holding On is a journey through the delicate, often bittersweet experiences that shape our lives. It is about the quiet, unspoken moments that define our relationships with others, ourselves, and the world around us. This collection explores what it means to hold on: to love, to grief, to memories, to hope, and ultimately, to life itself.

Holding on can be an act of strength—fingers grasping for connection, hearts clinging to the past, and spirits enduring through storms. But sometimes, it is the softest gesture that requires the most courage: the choice to embrace vulnerability, to allow ourselves to let go when needed, or to trust that holding on won't break us, but rather, heal us.

Each poem in this collection reflects a piece of that tender balance—how we carry love, loss, resilience, and change. These poems are whispers for the moments when words feel too heavy, and yet they are also meant to offer light for the path forward, for the days when you may find yourself holding on to hope, to love, to possibility.

This book is a tribute to those who continue to hold on, even when it feels impossible. It is a recognition of the strength in fragility, the beauty in persistence, and the grace in letting things unfold as they may.

Wherever this collection finds you, may you see yourself in these pages, and may you discover that holding on is an art that we all learn, one tender moment at a time.

Part 1: Love & Connection

Fingers Intertwined

In the quiet space between our palms,
Our fingers meet like roots in soil,
Twisting, tangling, soft and warm,
A gesture gentle, yet never spoiled.
With every squeeze, a promise made,
Of trust that lingers, of love conveyed,
No words needed, no voices loud,
In this touch, we're free, unbowed.
Your hand in mine, a quiet vow,
A bond that time cannot unplow,
Though storms may come and winds may tear,
We hold on tight, for we still care.
The world fades soft, the night draws near,
But fingers intertwined, there's no fear.

Hands Collide

In the moment our hands collide,
The world shrinks down, no need to hide,
Your touch a language, soft and sweet,
A rhythm that makes my heart skip beats.
Fingers twisted, trust enclosed,
A space where fear is never exposed,
I hold you close in this embrace,
Two hearts, one rhythm, one quiet place.
The smallest movement speaks of care,
In the silent grip we bravely share,
A fragile thing, this bond of ours,
Yet stronger than the tallest towers.
Together, we'll weather, we'll fight, we'll find—
All we need are fingers intertwined.

Fleeting Touch

In this fleeting touch, so pure,
We find a way to endure,
When words fail, and time grows still,
Your hand in mine becomes our will.
Every crease and line we meet,
A story lived, complete, yet sweet,
In the space between, we mend,
What was broken, we defend.
With every thread of trust and care,
We build a world that's light as air,
But strong enough to hold us tight,
Through every storm and darkened night.
Fingers intertwined, we stay,
No words, just hands that show the way.

Beneath the Stars

Beneath the sky, beneath the stars,
Our hands align like falling sparks,
In this quiet, fleeting dance,
I find myself in your gentle glance.
Fingers meet like rivers merge,
A tender tide, a silent surge,
No need for speeches, nor grand display,
Just the touch that lights the way.
We hold the world within this clasp,
Each breath, a promise that we grasp,
Through the silence, through the noise,
Fingers hold what words destroy.
In this embrace, we find what's true,
My fingers intertwined with you.

Simple Grace

Your hand in mine, a simple grace,
Yet here we find our quiet place,
A refuge built from skin and bone,
Where neither heart is left alone.
With every clasp, with every squeeze,
We lock away our greatest fears,
In this touch, we've learned to trust,
To hold on tight when life feels rushed.
Our fingers thread, like roots they grow,
In this small space, we feel the glow,
Of love that whispers, soft yet clear,
A language only we can hear.
Fingers intertwined, we see,
In this embrace, we're wild and free.

Beneath the Weight

Beneath the weight of all we know,
Our hands entwine, and let love flow,
No need for words to calm the storm,
This touch alone keeps us warm.
Fingers find their way with ease,
Through tangled paths of memories,
Each crease, a journey long and deep,
Each touch, a promise we will keep.
In this grip, both strong and light,
We hold each other through the night,
Fingers locked, hearts intertwined,
In this touch, our souls aligned.
No fear, no doubt, just us two,
Fingers intertwined, we make it through.

Silent Symphony

A kiss arrives without a sound,
Yet speaks a language of its own,
In whispered breaths and softest touch,
It holds a world, so much, so much.
Between our lips, a thousand words,
No need for voices to be heard,
In this brief moment, time stands still,
The world bends softly to our will.
A silent symphony we share,
A kiss that lingers in the air.

In the Space Between

The space between us fades away,
As lips collide, our fears decay,
In this small moment, worlds collide,
A touch where all our dreams reside.
A fleeting spark, a gentle sigh,
Yet more profound than meets the eye,
In this exchange, our hearts align,
A kiss that speaks of love divine.
It's here we find what words can't say—
In one brief kiss, we melt away.

The Breath of Us

In the breath that follows touch,
A kiss can feel like far too much,
It holds the weight of love and care,
A silent promise hanging there.
The brush of lips, so soft, so sweet,
A place where love and passion meet,
It lingers long beyond the night,
A kiss that keeps the soul alight.
In every breath, we breathe anew,
A kiss that whispers, "I see you."

Of Time and Tenderness

A kiss can freeze the world in place,
Can soften time, can slow the race,
In just a moment, all is clear,
No future, past—just you, right here.
The gentle press of lips to skin,
Is where the greatest truths begin,
A touch that holds a universe,
A love unspoken, unrehearsed.
In tenderness, our hearts confess,
The weight of love in one caress.

A World in Waiting

A kiss, a pause, the world on edge,
A delicate and trembling pledge,
It holds the hope of what could be,
The weight of love yet still unseen.
In this brief moment, time suspends,
Two hearts unsure of how it ends,
Yet in the stillness, passion sways,
A kiss that holds a thousand ways.
In one small touch, we start anew,
A kiss that promises the truth.

Echoes in the Dark

A kiss that blooms in midnight air,
Is more than love, it's more than care,
It carries with it every fear,
And every hope we hold so near.
In darkness, we are still exposed,
A kiss that lingers, softly glows,
It echoes through the quiet night,
A spark that keeps the heart alight.
In shadows deep, it shows the way—
A kiss that brings the light of day.

Ink Without a Destination

I wrote your name a thousand times,
Across the pages of my mind,
In letters I could never send,
Fearing how the words might end.
Each line a truth I couldn't say,
For what if you should turn away?
So ink remained, a quiet plea,
A secret locked, just you and me.
These pages bear the weight of fear,
The love I held, I held so near.
But every word stayed trapped inside,
A whisper lost, a heart denied.
And though the paper longs to speak,
The courage I could never seek.

Between the Lines

The letters sit, unsent, unread,
Words caught between my heart and head,
Each sentence draped in quiet care,
But left in silence, hanging there.
The space between the words I write,
Holds every hope, holds every fright,
For once they fly, there's no return,
A love that risks to crash and burn.
So here they stay, between the lines,
A love unspoken, undefined,
I wish I knew what you would say,
If these frail words could find their way.
But fear, it holds me fast in place—
And words are lost without a trace.

The Weight of Silence

The weight of silence fills the page,
Where every word remains encaged,
I write you letters late at night,
But none escape the paper's sight.
For what if love, once shared, would fade?
What if these words brought only shade?
So here they rest, a quiet plea,
A story never meant to be.
I fold the paper, tuck it tight,
Away from day, away from light,
A secret left within my chest,
A truth that never will confess.
These letters, born from love's intent,
Are bound to stay—forever sent.

The Postmarks of My Heart

I drafted words in morning light,
In hopes they'd see the world tonight,
But every stroke, each tender plea,
Fell short of courage's decree.
I traced your name, I signed my own,
But something in me felt alone,
Afraid of how the truth might land,
If you held these words in your hand.
So every postmark in my mind,
Stayed locked in fears I couldn't find,
And though I longed for you to know,
The fear of loss held back the flow.
Each letter, sealed in love's attempt,
Became a note I never sent.

What Could Have Been

Each letter that I never mailed,
Is part of love I never hailed,
For every line unsent, unread,
Is part of what we could have said.
The words I wrote in fleeting fire,
Became a tale of lost desire,
A dream that never saw the light,
A love that never had its flight.
These words remain a haunting thought,
Of all the things we never sought,
And in the silence of each fold,
Is where the truth remains untold.
The letters never found their way,
And now, the love begins to fray.

Whispers in the Envelope

I sealed the envelope with care,
But never sent it anywhere,
The words inside so full of you,
But doubt, it held the final view.
For love unsaid is safer still,
Than love that tumbles down a hill,
So every letter finds its place,
In drawers filled with empty space.
The ink, though dry, still lingers here,
The hopes I held, the buried fear,
And though my heart cries out to speak,
The silence keeps me soft and meek.
These letters never crossed the line,
And now they fade with passing time.

Whispers in the Wind

Your name still drifts upon the air,
A whisper soft, beyond compare,
Though time has passed and you've moved on,
The echo of you isn't gone.
In quiet moments, when I dream,
It lingers like a distant stream,
A sound so faint, yet crystal clear,
Your name, once love, still hovers near.
I call it back, though none can hear,
It carries all I once held dear,
Like wind through leaves, it softly flows,
A love remembered, though it goes.
Your name, a song that doesn't fade,
Still fills the silence we once made.

Faded Letters

Your name was once a song I spoke,
A melody that softly broke,
Upon my lips, with every breath,
Now echoes linger after death.
The letters blur, the sound grows faint,
Yet in my heart, your name's a saint,
A ghost that haunts the space between,
What is, what was, what might have been.
Though years have passed, I still recall,
The way your name could hold it all,
And even now, when silence reigns,
I hear it whispered through the panes.
Your name is written on my soul,
An echo that will never dull.

A Shadow in the Rain

Your name returns with every storm,
A shadow in the rain, still warm,
Though you are gone, it finds its way,
To me, in moments of dismay.
I hear it in the patter soft,
Like memories I've tucked aloft,
The way you used to call to me,
Is carried still by winds set free.
And though the years have drawn apart,
Your name still sings inside my heart,
An echo that won't fade away,
No matter how I try to sway.
A shadow traced in falling rain,
Your name, forever in my veins.

Carved in Stone

Your name is carved where none can see,
A quiet place, inside of me,
Though time erodes what once was bright,
It stays, still etched, in fading light.
Each syllable, once full of grace,
Now lingers in this hollow space,
A sound that once was love's refrain,
Now echoes softly, still the same.
I speak it when the world is still,
And feel its echo like a chill,
For though you've gone and life moves on,
Your name remains when all is gone.
Carved deep within, it doesn't change,
Your name, forever rearranged.

In Every Quiet Room

Your name still hangs in empty halls,
A sound that rises, then it falls,
It fills the quiet with its hum,
A gentle ache that doesn't numb.
In every quiet room I find,
Your name returns, still intertwined,
With memories that once were bright,
Now lingering in fading light.
No matter how I turn away,
Your name returns, it cannot stray,
It lives in every breath I take,
An echo of the love we'd make.
Though distance grows and years decay,
Your name within me finds its way.

In the Space Between

Your name is in the space between,
The moments where I sit and dream,
A sound that fills the cracks of time,
Like whispered notes of distant chimes.
It echoes soft in morning's glow,
And follows me wherever I go,
Though silence rules the world I see,
Your name still whispers back to me.
Each syllable, a tender ghost,
Of what we cherished, loved the most,
Though you are gone, the sound remains,
A soft refrain through joy and pain.
In every space, in every dream,
Your name still echoes, though unseen.

Tangled in the Wind

There are threads we cannot see,
Spun between both you and me,
Tangled in the wind they sway,
Yet always find their certain way.
Through distance wide or time that fades,
These threads remain, though colors shade,
A bond we feel but cannot hold,
Invisible yet brave and bold.
When silence falls, and we're apart,
They pull us closer, heart to heart,
No force of nature can undo,
What threads of love have tied us to.
And so we move, and so we stay,
These threads are with us, come what may.

The Weaving of Souls

Unseen by eyes, yet felt by soul,
The threads between us make us whole,
Woven deep in quiet night,
They bind us close, though out of sight.
Through years and miles, they do not break,
A pull so strong, no storm could shake,
These threads of trust and love so fine,
Tie your heart forever to mine.
Though hands may never touch the strands,
They weave through life like gentle hands,
Guiding us to where we belong,
A tether that's been there all along.
Invisible, yet always known,
These threads remind us we're not alone.

Beyond the Eye

The threads between us shimmer bright,
Though hidden far beyond our sight,
They stretch across both time and space,
And tie us in their soft embrace.
Each thread a moment shared, unseen,
Each bond a place where love has been,
They carry whispers through the air,
And hold us close when we're not there.
Though miles may keep us far apart,
These threads still reach from heart to heart,
No distance long, no silence deep,
Can break what these connections keep.
Beyond the eye, beyond the hand,
These threads between us understand.

Tied by the Quiet

In quiet moments, I can feel,
The threads that tie us, soft yet real,
They hum beneath the noise of life,
A silent bond, immune to strife.
Invisible, yet strong and clear,
They pull us close, despite the fear,
When all seems lost, and hope has flown,
These threads remind we're not alone.
They stretch through time, they span the years,
A comfort woven from our tears,
Tied by love, and tied by trust,
They hold us firm when all seems dust.
Though unseen by the naked eye,
These threads of ours will never die.

The Fabric of Connection

We're stitched together, you and I,
With threads that none can see or tie,
A fabric made of laughter, tears,
Woven through both joy and fears.
Each thread a moment, light or dark,
A bond that leaves its subtle mark,
And though the fabric frays with time,
These threads still hold, soft and sublime.
They weave through nights when we're apart,
And bind us close from heart to heart,
Unseen by those who watch and stare,
But felt in every breath of air.
The fabric of connection, sewn,
Is where our deepest love is known.

A Tether of Light

There's a tether between you and me,
Invisible, yet wild and free,
A line of light that stretches far,
Guiding us, a northern star.
Through darkened nights and stormy seas,
This tether pulls with gentle ease,
No matter how far we may drift,
It brings us back, a timeless gift.
We feel it when we speak in dreams,
Or in the quiet moments' seams,
A thread so thin, yet shining bright,
It holds us fast in love's true light.
This tether, though you cannot see,
Is always here, connecting me to thee.

Silent Conversations

We speak without a single word,
No voice, no sound, no thought disturbed,
For in the silence, we are whole,
Each breath a whisper of the soul.
Beneath the skin, our truths reside,
Where all our fears and hopes collide,
You know me in a way so rare,
A depth beyond what words could share.
Your glance reveals what's left unsaid,
Your touch, a map where love is read,
In every pause, we find the way,
To speak the things we dare not say.
No need for language, loud or clear,
Our hearts converse, for you are near.

The Language of Touch

Your hand upon my skin reveals,
A language only touch can feel,
No need for words, for what we know,
Exists in places words can't go.
Beneath the surface, deep and true,
I feel the way you understand too,
In every gesture, soft yet strong,
We speak a language all our own.
The way your hand rests upon mine,
Tells stories far beyond the line,
Of what is seen or spoken here—
It whispers love, both loud and clear.
In every quiet touch, I see,
The silent way you speak to me.

Where Eyes Meet

When our eyes meet, the world dissolves,
And something deeper soon evolves,
A bond that's made in quiet glances,
Where every fear and hope advances.
Beneath the skin, beyond the gaze,
We move through life's most tender maze,
With just a look, I feel your heart,
No words required to play their part.
For in your eyes, I see my home,
A place where I am not alone,
You speak to me in ways so rare,
A silent love, beyond compare.
The world may speak in endless cries,
But we, we talk where silence lies.

The Unspoken Realm

We move through life without the need,
For words that others might misread,
For what we share is far below,
The surface where most people go.
In quiet moments, you are there,
A presence felt beyond the air,
Beneath the skin, you understand,
The things I never planned to hand.
Our love exists in silent streams,
In whispered thoughts and unseen dreams,
Where every glance and every touch,
Says far too little, yet so much.
We need no voice to make it real,
For what we have, we simply feel.

In Every Breath

In every breath we share a word,
Unspoken, yet it's always heard,
A quiet pulse beneath the skin,
Where all the truest truths begin.
You know me in a way so deep,
Where secrets rest and shadows sleep,
Your presence hums inside my bones,
A quiet love that softly grows.
Beneath the skin, beyond the air,
Is where we find our meaning there,
Without the noise of sound or speech,
We touch what others cannot reach.
In every breath, in every space,
I feel your love, a warm embrace.

The Quiet Knowing

In the quiet knowing, we reside,
A love that's never tried to hide,
For what we are, beneath the skin,
Is where the deepest truths begin.
You sense my soul before I speak,
You lift me when I'm feeling weak,
Without a word, without a sound,
You hold me when the world spins 'round.
Your understanding, soft and clear,
Whispers all the things I fear,
And in return, I give to you,
A love that's silent, but so true.
We do not need the noise of voice,
For what we share has made its choice.

Part 2: Grief & Letting Go

Whispers of What Was

How do you hold a ghost in hand,
When all that's left is fading sand?
The touch that once could calm my fears,
Now lives in shadows, lives in tears.
I reach for you in quiet air,
But find there's nothing really there,
Just echoes of the life we knew,
And memories I cling onto.
The way you smiled, the things you'd say,
Still linger though you've gone away,
I hold you in the fading light,
A ghost that walks with me at night.
Though time may soften grief's sharp edge,
I still hold you, upon a ledge.

Carrying the Silence

How do I carry you, now gone?
In moments where the world moves on?
Your laughter, once a steady guide,
Now lives in silence, just outside.
I hold you in the quiet hours,
Like petals pressed from faded flowers,
A memory too soft to grasp,
Yet one I'll never dare unclasp.
Each step I take, I feel you near,
A ghost who whispers through the fear,
You linger just beyond my reach,
A lesson time will never teach.
How to live without your touch—
I hold the silence all too much.

Shadows in the Light

You walk beside me, though unseen,
A shadow in the space between,
Where sunlight falls and memories hide,
You stay with me, still by my side.
Though you have left, you're never far,
Your presence shines like a distant star,
I hold the ghost of who you were,
A quiet hum, a gentle blur.
I speak your name when night is deep,
And dream of you in every sleep,
Your shadow slips through every day,
Though time tries hard to pull away.
I hold you in the smallest things,
A ghost that every sunrise brings.

The Weight of Air

You've become the weight of air,
A presence felt, though never there,
A ghost I carry every day,
Though you have slowly slipped away.
I hold you in the space between,
Where dreams exist and truth is seen,
Your laughter fills the silent room,
A flower lost, still in bloom.
And though I cannot touch your face,
I feel you in this empty space,
A whisper soft, a shadow small,
But you are here, within it all.
The weight of air, so light, yet known—
A ghost I carry as my own.

In the Quiet Corners

You linger in the quiet corners,
Where light refracts and slowly borders,
The edges of the life I lead,
A ghost, invisible, yet freed.
I hold you in the broken places,
In memories, in empty spaces,
Your voice still echoes, soft, serene,
A ghost that lives in what's unseen.
I reach for you, though you're long gone,
The tender art of moving on,
Is learning how to let you stay,
While life continues day by day.
In corners where the shadows play,
Your ghost still lives, though far away.

The Ghost That Time Won't Heal

Time tells me that you're fading fast,
But still, I hold onto the past,
A ghost that time cannot erase,
You linger here in every place.
I feel your touch in gentle rain,
Your voice is in the winds that wane,
I hold you close in every song,
A ghost I've carried all along.
Though grief may soften, love remains,
A ghost that's woven in my veins,
You slip through time, you fill my heart,
In ways that time can't pull apart.
The ghost of you, I keep, I hold—
Your memory, forever gold.

Echoes in the Silence

The space you left is wide and deep,
A silence where your voice would sleep,
Each room now holds a hollow sound,
Where once your laughter danced around.
I walk through echoes of your days,
And every shadow softly sways,
As if you've just stepped out of sight,
But never far, not quite, not quite.
Grief fills the void where you once stood,
A weight that's heavy, yet understood.

Empty Corners

The corners of the house feel cold,
Where once your presence was so bold,
Now every space is stretched too thin,
Grief settles like the air within.
Your chair sits still, untouched, alone,
A monument of all you've known,
I reach for you in every room,
But all I find is quiet gloom.
The empty space is loud and clear,
Grief fills it with the weight of fear.

A Void That Grows

The space you left behind has grown,
A void I've slowly come to own,
It stretches wide with every day,
As pieces of you fade away.
Grief fills the cracks where love once stood,
It ebbs and flows, misunderstood,
A hollow ache that breathes and bends,
That shifts and shapes but never ends.
The space you left becomes my guide,
A place where sorrow learns to hide.

Silent Walls

The walls that once heard all your words,
Now stand in silence, undisturbed,
They miss the way you used to speak,
The stories shared, the voice unique.
Now grief has taken up the space,
Where joy once danced with easy grace,
Each memory now bittersweet,
A fragile love that feels complete.
The space you left will always stay,
A home for grief to softly lay.

Hollow Places

The hollow places where you were,
Now echo like a whispered blur,
I reach for you in empty air,
But find that grief has settled there.
The space you left behind is vast,
A haunting echo of the past,
It fills with sorrow, slow and sure,
A grief that's tender, hard to cure.
The emptiness is not unkind—
It's simply what you left behind.

The Absence You Became

The absence you became is clear,
A space where love still lingers near,
But grief has found a way to grow,
In places only you would know.
The empty chair, the quiet hall,
Each one reminds me of it all,
Your absence fills the house with sound,
Of memories no longer found.
The space you left is still, refined,
A home for grief, now redefined.

The Space Between Our Hands

Your hands no longer reach for mine,
A touch now lost to the sands of time,
Yet still, I feel you in the air,
As though your presence lingers there.
I reach for you in moments still,
But find the emptiness I fill,
A hand that once could calm my fear,
Now just a memory held near.
Though distance grows, though you have flown,
Your touch remains in ways unknown,
I feel it in the quiet night,
In every dream, you hold me tight.
The space between our hands is wide,
But still, I feel you by my side.

Where Hands Once Met

Your hands, once warm, once strong and kind,
Are now a memory in my mind,
I reach for you, but nothing's there,
Just whispers caught within the air.
Those hands that held me in my pain,
That promised me through sun and rain,
Have slipped beyond my earthly reach,
Yet still, your lessons softly teach.
I carry you in every step,
In every breath, your love is kept,
Though hands no longer clasp in place,
I feel your fingers brush my face.
In shadows where your hands once met,
You linger still—I won't forget.

The Ghost of Your Touch

Your hands no longer reach for me,
Yet still, their ghost won't let me be,
I feel them in the morning light,
A phantom touch, both soft and bright.
The way you'd hold me, hold me close,
Those moments are what haunt me most,
For though I cannot touch you now,
Your love still shows me where and how.
Your hands, though gone, still guide my way,
Through every dark and broken day,
I feel them in the breeze at night,
A gentle touch that feels so right.
Though I may never hold you near,
Your hands remain, forever here.

Beyond the Reach of Time

Your hands, once full of love and care,
Now rest beyond the world we share,
I reach for you in fleeting dreams,
But find you just beyond the seams.
Your touch, a memory now lost,
Yet worth whatever it may cost,
For though you've slipped from mortal grasp,
Your hands still hold me in their clasp.
Through moments when I feel alone,
I sense your fingers, though they've flown,
They pull me close, they lift me high,
Like wings that carry me to sky.
Your hands no longer reach in time,
But still, they guide this heart of mine.

The Hands I Cannot Hold

The hands I cannot hold again,
Once filled with strength, with love, with pain,
Now drift away like autumn leaves,
Yet in their loss, my heart still grieves.
I reach, I stretch, I call your name,
But distance now is not the same,
Your hands, once warm, now feel so far,
Yet still, they guide me like a star.
I hold the thought of you so tight,
Your hands, still there, though out of sight,
And in the quiet of my mind,
Your fingers hold me, soft and kind.
Though hands no longer meet in space,
Their memory, I still embrace.

Hands Across the Veil

Your hands, now gone, are out of reach,
Yet in their absence, they still teach,
They hold me through the darkest night,
They guide me toward the softest light.
Though I can no longer feel their touch,
Their absence speaks of love so much,
A love that crosses time and space,
That lives beyond the human race.
I reach for you in empty air,
And find your presence everywhere,
Your hands, though gone, still pull me near,
Their warmth is what I feel most clear.
Across the veil, I feel you stay—
Your hands still hold me every day.

Incomplete Farewells

The last goodbye was soft, unsure,
A whisper fading, still impure,
For though the words were meant to end,
It felt like more was left to mend.
You turned to go, but lingered still,
As if your heart resisted will,
And in that moment, all we said,
Was drowned by silence, thick as lead.
Some goodbyes never find their way,
They hang in air, too scared to stay,
A final word that drifts like smoke,
Unfinished lines, too hard to choke.
The last goodbye, it never ends—
It echoes where the silence bends.

A Farewell Left Unsaid

There was no word, no final speech,
No parting thought I tried to reach,
You simply left, without a sound,
No closing line, no solid ground.
I stood there, waiting for the phrase,
That might release me from this maze,
But all I found was empty air,
A quiet loss too much to bear.
Some goodbyes hide within the cracks,
Of time and space, no turning back,
And though you're gone, I still remain,
In search of what we never named.
A farewell left unsaid is worse—
It leaves the heart beneath a curse.

The Weight of Goodbye

The weight of saying one last word,
Is heavy, though it's barely heard,
It lingers long after you leave,
A presence that makes hearts believe.
Goodbyes are never truly done,
They rest beneath the setting sun,
A shadow cast, a lingering breath,
That hovers just beyond the death.
Though you are gone, I feel you near,
Your last goodbye still whispers here,
Unfinished lines that haunt my mind,
A love too strong to leave behind.
The weight of parting words we keep,
Lives on in every silent sleep.

Unspoken Goodbyes

You didn't speak a single word,
But still, your absence can be heard,
In every room, in every sound,
A silence that is most profound.
The last goodbye was never said,
It lingers here inside my head,
A thought that's tethered to my heart,
A wound that time won't let depart.
Perhaps some farewells can't be told,
Too heavy for the tongue to hold,
So we leave them hanging in the air,
A silent grief we cannot share.
Unspoken goodbyes leave their mark,
A quiet echo in the dark.

The Door That Never Closed

I watched you leave, you walked away,
But something in you wished to stay,
A part of you that couldn't bear,
To fully leave what we once shared.
The door, ajar, a crack of light,
A sign that nothing ends just right,
Goodbyes, they linger like the breeze,
A soft farewell that never frees.
We try to close the final page,
But find ourselves inside the cage,
Of words unsaid and tears not cried,
Of moments when the soul still hides.
The door that never truly closed—
A goodbye left, but never posed.

The Lingering Goodbye

You said goodbye, but didn't mean,
The final weight of what you'd seen,
Your voice was soft, your eyes unsure,
As if you longed for something more.
Goodbyes that linger never end,
They twist and turn, they start to bend,
A parting word that won't stay still,
It haunts the heart against its will.
I hear your voice in every sigh,
A whisper, though you said goodbye,
For though we spoke those final lines,
The love we shared still intertwines.
Goodbyes, they linger, never gone—
They live in shadows, moving on.

Faded Edges

The edges of your memory blur,
A face I knew, no longer sure,
I reach for you in thoughts gone still,
But find the silence hard to fill.
What once was sharp, so full of light,
Now fades within the endless night,
I hold you close, but can't deny,
The passing years that slowly lie.
I try to grasp what still remains,
Yet time has slipped between the veins,
A fragile thing, this memory,
That dances just beyond the sea.
And so, I hold what I can keep—
A fading dream inside my sleep.

Cracks of Time

Through cracks of time, the moments fall,
So small, so silent, almost all,
The laughter once that filled the air,
Now drifts away, I'm unaware.
I chase the shadows of the past,
But find they're slipping far too fast,
I gather what I think I know,
Yet even that begins to go.
The hands of time are soft but strong,
They take what doesn't last for long,
And all that's left is what we hold,
So fragile, delicate, and bold.
The balance tips from time to time—
And memories fall, line by line.

The Weight of Memory

I hold the weight of what remains,
In fragments caught like falling rain,
A moment here, a thought of you,
But time erodes what once was true.
The years have softened every line,
The touch, the laugh, once yours and mine,
And though I hold you close in heart,
I fear the fading will soon start.
For memories are fragile things,
Like butterflies with brittle wings,
And though I try to keep them near,
They slip away, they disappear.
I carry what I can sustain,
But still, the loss runs through my veins.

Between the Shattered Glass

I pick the pieces, one by one,
Of memories now come undone,
Like shattered glass upon the floor,
I try to hold, but lose much more.
For every shard I lift with care,
Another slips into the air,
And though I gather all I can,
What's lost will never touch my hand.
The fragile bits that still remain,
Are filled with both delight and pain,
A mirror cracked by passing days,
That shows a face in distant haze.
Between the glass, I find your name—
A fragile love that feels the same.

What Time Won't Take

The fragile things are all we keep,
The memories we store so deep,
And yet, despite how hard we try,
They fade like stars in morning sky.
I cling to what still flickers here,
A smile, a voice, a whispered tear,
But time, it takes, it steals away,
The things we swore would always stay.
Yet still, I hold them in my palm,
The broken, tender, fragile calm,
Of love that once was wild and strong,
Now quiet, though it lingers long.
What time won't take, I hold in vain—
A fragile thing that still remains.

Fading Faces

I fear the day your face will fade,
Like sunlight lost in evening's shade,
When memories, once sharp and clear,
Slip softly out, and disappear.
The heart, so tender, holds its grip,
But time still makes its shadows drip,
I wonder if I'm letting go,
Of love I vowed to always know.
And in that loss, what will remain—
Just echoes of a passing name.

The Guilt of Moving On

I move ahead, but with a weight,
Of leaving you behind, too late,
Each step feels heavy, steeped in guilt,
For crossing bridges that we built.
The world expects that time will heal,
But love is something you still feel,
And moving forward feels untrue,
As if I'm letting go of you.
How do I live and still hold dear,
The love we shared, while you're not here?

The Fading Name

Your name, once whispered every day,
Now drifts like clouds, too far away,
I speak it softly in the dark,
But fear it's losing its old spark.
The heart forgets, despite its fight,
Memories dim with fading light,
And though I try to keep you near,
Each day you seem to disappear.
I dread the moment when I find,
Your name no longer in my mind.

Letting Go, Holding On

There's guilt in every forward step,
As if my heart should only weep,
And though I know you're always here,
The fear of loss is ever near.
Forgetting feels like losing twice,
Like paying love a heavy price,
Yet still, the world won't let me stay,
In sorrow's grip, day after day.
So I move forward, though it stings,
Afraid of all forgetting brings.

Echoes of What Was

The echoes of you fade away,
A little more with every day,
And though I try to make you stay,
I feel you slowly slip astray.
The heart forgets despite its will,
A quiet loss that haunts me still,
For moving on feels like a crime,
A theft against the hands of time.
I hold you close, but still I fear,
That soon you'll fade beyond the years.

Part 3: Self & Inner Strength

A Heavy Grip

I hold on tight, though time has passed,
To something fragile, built to last,
Yet now it's worn, it's lost its glow,
But still, I can't quite let it go.
The weight of love, of all we were,
Hangs heavy, like a whispered blur,
I carry it through every day,
Though part of me has slipped away.
Is holding on a sign of strength?
Or does it drain me at length?
For what I grasp is old and thin,
A past I feel beneath my skin.
Yet still, I bear its quiet load,
The weight of what can't be bestowed.

The Cost of Clinging

I hold onto the faded threads,
Of what once bloomed but now lies dead,
The weight of things that no longer bloom,
Yet still, I carry in this room.
To let it go would be release,
But holding on feels like a peace,
A way to honour what once was,
To give it more than just because.
But every day, I feel the strain,
Of holding on to all this pain,
A heaviness I wear each day,
That keeps the light so far away.
And yet I cling, for fear that loss,
Will be a burden twice the cost.

Beneath the Surface

I carry things beneath the skin,
The weight of what has always been,
A love, a hurt, a silent plea,
To hold on tight, despite the sea.
But now, the waves begin to rise,
And yet, I can't release the ties,
I cling to moments long since gone,
To feelings that should not go on.
The burden's light, but still it grows,
It binds me where the river flows,
I cannot swim, I cannot breathe,
Yet still, I hold and do not leave.
The weight of what I can't release,
Steals every breath, denies me peace.

The Quiet Burden

The quiet burden of this grip,
Is something I cannot let slip,
Though what I hold has lost its power,
I carry it through every hour.
It pulls me back when I might rise,
It clouds my thoughts, it fills my skies,
But still, I hold, though I don't know,
What clinging serves, where I must go.
I fear that letting go would break,
The things that make my soul awake,
So I endure this heavy load,
And walk alone on this old road.
For sometimes, holding on too long,
Can make us forget we are strong.

The Weight of Yesterday

Yesterday, it pulls me down,
A heavy weight that makes me drown,
I clutch it close, though it's a chain,
That binds me tight, that brings me pain.
The past, it holds a certain grace,
A memory I can't erase,
Yet as I cling, I feel the cost,
Of all that's been, of all that's lost.
The weight of holding on is clear,
It steals the present, makes me fear,
That moving forward might betray,
The things I carried from that day.
But still, I cling, though hands grow weak,
For in this burden, love still speaks.

The Courage of Release

To hold on tight, it takes such strength,
To carry love through endless length,
But there's a courage just as true,
In letting go, in starting new.
The weight of what we try to keep,
Can often steal our need to leap,
For holding on to what once was,
Can trap us in a long because.
I feel the weight, I feel it press,
A quiet strain of tenderness,
Yet part of me begins to see,
That letting go might set me free.
The weight of holding on is hard,
But release is its own reward.

The Anchor and the Chain

I hold on tight to what remains,
An anchor bound by rusted chains,
Though what I cling to pulls me down,
I fear release might let me drown.
This weight, it presses on my chest,
But somehow feels like needed rest,
A burden I have learned to bear,
A quiet load I do not share.
To let it go, to set it free,
Would be a loss I cannot see,
For in the heavy, there is peace,
A comfort found in the release.
Yet still, I wonder what it means,
To carry pasts like shadowed dreams.

Grasping at Shadows

I clutch the shadows of the past,
Though none of them were built to last,
They slip between my trembling hands,
Like grains of sand from distant lands.
The weight of what I can't let go,
Keeps me tethered, moving slow,
I try to pull the pieces near,
But find them fading year by year.
To hold so tight to what is gone,
Is living in a world withdrawn,
A place where light can barely reach,
And every touch is out of reach.
Still, I grip the fleeting night,
Afraid of losing all the light.

The Hands That Never Loosen

My hands, they ache from holding tight,
To love that's faded from my sight,
Yet still I cling, as if to prove,
That letting go would mean I lose.
The weight of all the years we shared,
The quiet moments when you cared,
They sit upon my weary heart,
A heaviness that won't depart.
But holding on is not the same,
As keeping you within a frame,
For time will twist and time will fade,
And every bond we had will fray.
Still, my hands refuse to part—
From the echo of your heart.

The Quiet Weight of Love

The weight of love, it whispers low,
A burden only we can know,
It settles deep within the soul,
And makes us feel both full and whole.
But sometimes love can be a stone,
A heavy thing we bear alone,
A memory that lingers long,
A song that never finds its song.
To carry love when it has died,
Is keeping something deep inside,
That drags us down and holds us still,
A heart that never has its fill.
Yet even as it strains and slows,
The weight of love is all we know.

Silent Resistance

The world pulls hard, it wants my soul,
To shape, to twist, to take control,
But in the silence, I remain,
A quiet fight that knows no pain.
I hold on tight to who I am,
Despite the push, despite the slam,
Of voices trying to define,
The boundaries of this heart of mine.
In every step, I stand my ground,
A quiet fight without a sound.

Against the Tide

The current tries to pull me down,
To drown my voice without a sound,
But in the depths, I find my fight,
A spark that flickers in the night.
The world may push, may pull away,
But here I stand, and here I stay,
With quiet strength beneath the storm,
I hold my shape, I keep my form.
No noise, no scream, just steady grace—
A quiet fight that holds its place.

The Armour of Stillness

I wear my silence like a shield,
A quiet armour, never healed,
For every time the world demands,
I stand with calm, unshaken hands.
They shout, they push, they try to bend,
But I am not so quick to send,
Myself into the fray they seek—
I find my power in the weak.
For strength is often still and small,
A quiet fight that conquers all.

The Strength Within

The fight I carry is my own,
A battle fought but never shown,
The world may rage, may tear apart,
But I defend my inner heart.
With every test, with every blow,
I gather all I need to grow,
No need to scream, no need to shout,
I hold my strength from deep without.
For in the quiet lies the fight,
A steady heart that knows it's right.

The Push and Pull of Love

The heart is a muscle, it bends, it breaks,
It learns from every risk it takes,
It stretches wide when love is near,
And contracts small in times of fear.
It pulls in tight when loss is felt,
But with each tear, it starts to melt,
The weight it holds in grief or joy,
Is how it learns to heal, deploy.
For every beat that shakes its core,
The heart grows strong, endures much more,
It holds on tight when needed most,
And let's go when it feels the ghost.
In every tear and tender bruise,
The heart learns what it cannot lose.

Building Strength in Letting Go

The heart is a muscle that holds its weight,
Through love that lingers, through loss and fate,
It grows with every learned release,
Finding strength in quiet peace.
It doesn't shrink when it lets go,
But builds itself through ebb and flow,
For holding on to all that's past,
Can break the heart that wants to last.
So it learns when to hold, when to release,
To find its center, to find its peace,
The tug of war inside its walls,
Makes it stronger through every fall.
For every time it dares to try,
The heart grows stronger, beats more high.

The Heart Learns Grace

The heart is a muscle, it learns with grace,
To hold on tight, yet give things space,
It stretches wide with every tear,
And grows resilient through despair.
It knows the art of clinging close,
Of holding on when needed most,
Yet learns to soften, learn to mend,
When time and healing must ascend.
The heart knows strength in every beat,
In moments bitter and moments sweet,
It flexes with each love it finds,
And loosens where it must unwind.
The heart is stronger when it knows—
To hold on fast, and when to let go.

The Calm Within the Storm

The waves crash hard against my shore,
Each one stronger than before,
They pull me under, drag me down,
But still, I fight to never drown.
In every storm, I find a breath,
A quiet space that staves off death,
Where peace can come, though chaos reigns,
And strength is found despite the chains.
I pause between the rolling tides,
To find the calm that still resides,
It's in that moment, deep and clear,
Where fear subsides and courage nears.
A breath between the storm's assault,
Is where I find my inner vault.

Carving Space Amid the Chaos

The world spins fast, the seas run wild,
The waves rise up, relentless, riled,
I feel the pull beneath my feet,
The endless churn of life's defeat.
But somewhere in the deepest part,
I feel a pause inside my heart,
A breath that holds the world at bay,
A quiet stillness in the fray.
In that brief moment, strength returns,
The fire within begins to burn,
For in the pause between each wave,
I find the power to be brave.
And though the storms will always come,
I breathe between and overcome.

The Power of the Pause

The waves come fast, the storm rolls in,
A tide that pulls beneath my skin,
I fight to stand, to hold my ground,
But feel the weight of being bound.
Yet in the swirl of crashing sea,
I find a breath that sets me free,
A pause, a moment, brief and still,
Where I regain my fading will.
For life is not just storm and strife,
But learning how to breathe through life,
To find the strength between each gust,
To rise again when all is dust.
A breath between the waves that pound,
Is where I find I'm not yet drowned.

The Weight You Learn to Hold

I've learned to carry all I feel,
To bear the weight that life reveals,
Each burden resting on my back,
A heavy load, but I don't crack.
Self-reliance builds a wall,
Yet in its strength, I feel the call,
To let the world see what I bear,
And show the scars I hide with care.
For even as I carry strong,
The weight is heavy, it feels wrong,
To always hold without release,
To never let my heart find peace.
So I balance strength and soft descent,
And find a way to let it vent.

Carving Strength from Silence

I carry all I've never said,
The weight of thoughts that fill my head,
The quiet burdens, deep inside,
That none can see, though hard I've tried.
I lift them high, I walk alone,
Self-reliance, carved in bone,
But in my silence, cracks appear,
Revealing tender lines of fear.
For strength is not to hold too tight,
But knowing when to seek the light,
To let the weight of what I bear,
Be shared by those who truly care.
I carry much, but not in vain—
I find my strength in shared pain.

The Balance of Bearing

I walk with burdens on my chest,
A weight that never seems to rest,
I carry all the things I hide,
And let no one walk by my side.
Yet even as I bear this load,
I know I walk a narrow road,
For strength is not to stand alone,
But knowing when to let love be shown.
To carry all without a break,
Is to risk everything will shake,
And so I learn to let some go,
To balance strength with what I show.
For self-reliance can be strong,
But vulnerability belongs.

The Quiet Strength Within

I hold my weight with steady hands,
Though no one truly understands,
The things I carry deep inside,
The battles fought, the tears I've cried.
Self-reliance makes me whole,
A quiet strength that fills my soul,
Yet still, I know that even I,
Must let the world see when I cry.
For in the strength of what I bear,
There's room for softness, room to care,
And though I carry on alone,
I find the courage to be shown.
I balance weight and tender grace,
And find my strength in every space.

Part 4: Hope & Renewal

The Light Beyond Today

When today feels heavy, hard to bear,
And shadows linger everywhere,
I hold on tight, though skies are grey,
To the hope that tomorrow brings a way.
For every storm will one day break,
And in its wake, new dawns will wake,
The weight of now will lift and fly,
As light returns to fill the sky.
I hold on to the dream of more,
Of brighter days just past the door,
And even when the night seems long,
I find my strength in hope's sweet song.
Tomorrow waits, just out of sight,
I hold on tight, I seek its light.

Through the Darkness, Still I Stand

The weight of now may press me down,
But in my heart, I wear no crown,
Of sorrow's rule or hopeless reign,
For tomorrow calls me back again.
Though today may feel too much to bear,
I know that time is never fair,
And in the quiet, in the still,
Tomorrow waits beyond the hill.
I hold on to that distant shore,
Where light returns, where hope is more,
For every night must turn to day,
And all the shadows drift away.
Tomorrow holds what I can't see,
But I hold on to what will be.

A Glimmer Just Ahead

Today may feel like endless night,
But just ahead, there gleams a light,
A spark of hope I cannot see,
Yet still, it calls me quietly.
The weight of now may crush and strain,
But tomorrow whispers through the rain,
A promise that the sun will rise,
And clear the tears from heavy eyes.
I hold on to the thread so fine,
That ties tomorrow's hope to mine,
And even when the day feels long,
I hear tomorrow's softer song.
Tomorrow holds a brighter sky,
I hold on tight, I'll learn to fly.

The Promise of the Dawn

The sun may set in crimson red,
And fill my heart with heavy dread,
But I know that tomorrow's day,
Will chase the darkest clouds away.
For every end begins again,
A cycle that renews and mends,
And though today may test my heart,
Tomorrow offers a new start.
I hold on to the promise there,
That even in my deepest care,
Tomorrow brings a softer wind,
A chance to let my soul begin.
I hold on tight, I wait and trust,
That tomorrow brings what's fair and just.

Between the Storms

Today may shake my very core,
And leave me feeling lost once more,
But I know that tomorrow stands,
With open heart and open hands.
For every storm must find its end,
And every wound begins to mend,
And though today feels like a test,
Tomorrow offers time to rest.
I hold on to the hope that grows,
In every breeze the future blows,
And though today may tear me down,
Tomorrow waits without a frown.
The future calls with tender grace,
I hold on, and I find my place.

Holding On to Morning Light

The weight of now may pull me deep,
But I know hope does not sleep,
For somewhere in the morning light,
Tomorrow waits, just out of sight.
I hold on to its quiet call,
A promise that I won't let fall,
That even in the hardest days,
Tomorrow offers softer ways.
The light of dawn will soon appear,
And chase away today's last tear,
For every night must find its end,
And every heart, it learns to mend.
I hold on to that bright unknown—
Tomorrow's light will be my own.

The Light That Follows

The storm has passed, the skies are clear,
The dawn breaks bright, its light draws near,
The winds have stilled, the rain is gone,
And here begins the quiet dawn.
A golden hue begins to rise,
Painting hope across the skies,
The world, once shaken by the night,
Now breathes again in morning light.
The storm may rage, the night may fall,
But still, the sunrise conquers all,
For after darkness, light will grow,
A quiet strength we come to know.

The Dawn of Renewal

The night was long, the storm was wild,
But now the dawn is soft and mild,
The clouds have parted, washed away,
And here begins a brand new day.
The golden light begins to spread,
Bringing warmth where fear had tread,
The world, renewed, begins to shine,
A testament to time's design.
For even in the fiercest storm,
The sunrise brings a gentle form,
Of hope, resilience, and grace—
The beauty of a new day's face.

After the Tempest

The tempest tore the world apart,
It rattled windows, shook the heart,
But now the sky begins to glow,
A gentle light, a steady flow.
The storm has passed, the sky is wide,
And peace returns with morning's tide,
The colors bloom, the darkness fades,
As sunlight breaks through every shade.
For even after darkest hours,
The sunrise holds the healing powers,
To bring us back from what was lost,
And help us mend, no matter the cost.

The Quiet After

The storm is gone, the winds have died,
The sunrise spreads its arms so wide,
A canvas brushed with gold and pink,
A quiet pause, a chance to think.
The world, so shaken in the night,
Now breathes beneath the morning light,
Renewed, refreshed, alive once more,
The calm that follows every roar.
For in the silence, peace returns,
And from the storm, new strength we earn,
The sunrise shows what we can be—
Resilient, whole, and truly free.

A Gentle Flame

Hope flickers like a quiet flame,
Soft and small, yet not the same,
As other lights that burn too bright,
Hope is tender, pure, and light.
It whispers when the world is loud,
A fragile thing beneath the cloud,
That hovers over troubled days,
But still, it finds a thousand ways.
Though small, its warmth can touch the soul,
And piece by piece, make broken whole,
For hope, though gentle, holds a force,
That guides us on our winding course.
It carries us when strength has gone—
A gentle flame that leads us on.

Beneath the Weight of Fear

Hope lingers in the quiet space,
Beneath the weight of fear's embrace,
It's fragile, like a thread so fine,
Yet woven deep in every line.
Though storms may rage, and shadows creep,
Hope lies within us, tucked in deep,
A tender thought, a whispered dream,
That flows beneath the darkest stream.
It doesn't shout, it doesn't scream,
But softly lights a distant gleam,
A fragile spark that will not die,
No matter how the world may try.
For hope, though quiet, never yields,
It blooms like flowers in hidden fields.

The Soft Power of Hope

Hope doesn't come with mighty roar,
It doesn't crash upon the shore,
Instead, it's like the morning dew,
A quiet gift, forever new.
It rests upon the heart's despair,
A gentle touch, a whispered prayer,
That tells us we are not alone,
And finds us when the way's unknown.
Its strength is in its tender hold,
A force both fragile and yet bold,
For though it bends, it will not break,
It stands within the pain we make.
The softness of hope sustains the soul—
A quiet light that keeps us whole.

Beauty in the Broken

Between the cracks, where none would look,
A flower blooms, a quiet book,
Of strength and beauty born from stone,
In spaces where it grows alone.
The world may crush, the world may tear,
Yet something gentle rises there,
A bloom that bends but does not break,
A testament to what's at stake.
For in the places worn and scarred,
Where life has left the surface hard,
A bloom still finds its way to rise,
A small surprise beneath the skies.
Beauty thrives where hope is thin,
A bloom that blossoms deep within.

Roots in the Unseen

In the cracks where shadows play,
A bloom emerges through decay,
Its roots unseen, its struggle real,
Yet through the stone, it dares to heal.
Where others see a hardened wall,
It finds the strength to stand up tall,
A bloom that whispers, soft but strong,
That beauty finds where it belongs.
In every crack, in every tear,
A seed is born that's bold and rare,
A flower blooming out of sight,
Yet holding on with all its might.
For even in the darkest stone,
A bloom can rise, a world its own.

The Strength in Fragility

A bloom that rises from the cracks,
Knows nothing of the world it lacks,
It only knows to push and grow,
To seek the sun, to find its glow.
Though concrete walls may block its way,
It reaches out, it finds the day,
A fragile stem, a tender leaf,
Emerging through the world's belief.
That strength is not in what we see,
But what endures so quietly,
The flower blooms where others fail,
In places where the weak grow frail.
And in its bloom, a lesson shown—
That strength is more than stone on stone.

The Future in Our Hands

The future lies within our hands,
A world we shape, a place that stands,
Through every act of love we give,
Through kindness that helps others live.
Each touch, each gesture, builds a bridge,
Across the gaps, beyond the ridge,
Of fear, of doubt, that clouds our way,
But still, we rise to meet each day.
For in our hands, we hold the light,
That guides the future, burning bright,
And with our hearts, we plant the seeds,
Of hope and love, of future deeds.
Together, we can heal and grow—
The future blooms in what we sow.

A World Built by Love

The hands that hold the future close,
Are filled with love, the purest dose,
For every heart that dares to care,
Can shape a world beyond despair.
With kindness, we can lift the weight,
Of burdens that too often break,
And in our touch, we weave a thread,
That ties together hope long shed.
No act too small, no love too weak,
To build a world for those who seek,
A place where peace and joy can grow,
Where light shines through the darkest glow.
In every hand that dares to give,
The future's strength begins to live.

Hands That Build Tomorrow

In every hand, the future lies,
Beneath the weight of hopeful skies,
Each act of kindness that we show,
Is how tomorrow learns to grow.
For love is not a thing of dreams,
But what we build with steady streams,
Of care, compassion, holding tight,
To what we know will shape the light.
Together, we can heal the past,
With hands that hold the future fast,
Through gentle words and tender touch,
We give the world what it needs much.
The future waits within our care—
A world we build when love is there.

The Power in Our Hands

The hands that shape the world ahead,
Are those that give, that break the bread,
Of kindness shared, of love profound,
That lifts the lost, that spreads around.
For every hand that reaches out,
To heal the wounds, to calm the doubt,
Is building more than just today—
It shapes the world in every way.
The future waits within our grasp,
A thing we hold, a breath we clasp,
And when we love, the seeds take root,
Of peace and joy, of life's pursuit.
Together, we can change the tide—
The future grows with love as guide.

Disclaimer:

The poems in this book are works of artistic expression and personal reflection. While they explore themes of love, loss, grief, healing, and personal transformation, they are not intended to provide professional advice or guidance in dealing with emotional, psychological, or relational matters. The content is meant to evoke thought and emotion, offering an exploration of the human experience through poetry.

If you are experiencing emotional distress or mental health challenges, please seek support from a licensed professional, counsellor, or mental health expert. The author makes no claim to offer therapeutic solutions, and readers are encouraged to approach the content as art, not as instruction or advice.

Milton Keynes UK
Ingram Content Group UK Ltd.
UKHW042239011124
450424UK00001BA/98